THE AMERICAN GIRLS

 1764 KAYA, an adventurous Nez Perce girl whose deep love for horses and respect for nature nourish her spirit

 1774 FELICITY, a spunky, spritely colonial girl, full of energy and independence

 1824 JOSEFINA, a Hispanic girl whose heart and hopes are as big as the New Mexico sky

 1854 KIRSTEN, a pioneer girl of strength and spirit who settles on the frontier

 1864 ADDY, a courageous girl determined to be free in the midst of the Civil War

 1904 SAMANTHA, a bright Victorian beauty, an orphan raised by her wealthy grandmother

 1934 KIT, a clever, resourceful girl facing the Great Depression with spirit and determination

 1944 MOLLY, who schemes and dreams on the home front during World War Two

 1974 JULIE, a fun-loving girl from San Francisco who faces big changes—and creates a few of her own

1974
Julie
TELLS HER STORY

By MEGAN McDONALD

ILLUSTRATIONS ROBERT HUNT

VIGNETTES SUSAN McALILEY

★ American Girl®

Published by American Girl Publishing, Inc.
Copyright © 2007 by American Girl, LLC
All rights reserved. No part of this book may be used or reproduced in
any manner whatsoever without written permission except in the case of
brief quotations embodied in critical articles and reviews.

Questions or comments? Call 1-800-845-0005, visit **americangirl.com**,
or write to Customer Service, American Girl, 8400 Fairway Place,
Middleton, WI 53562-0497.

Printed in China
07 08 09 10 11 12 LEO 10 9 8 7 6 5 4 3 2 1

All American Girl marks, Julie™, and Julie Albright™
are trademarks of American Girl, LLC.

PICTURE CREDITS

The following individuals and organizations have generously given permission to reprint
images contained in "Looking Back": p. 31—used with permission of Universal Studios (Jaws
poster); p. 66—KerPlunk!® and associated trademarks and trade dress owned by and used
with permission of Mattel, Inc., © 2006 Mattel, Inc. All rights reserved; pp. 80–81—used with
permission of the California Clock Company (Kit-Cat clock); © Bettmann/Corbis (1970s
classroom); © JLP/Jose Luis Pelaez/zefa/Corbis (students with test tubes); courtesy of
Kathy Madison (ditto); © Christopher Stevenson/zefa/Corbis (typewriter); reprinted with
permission of Scholastic Inc. (Jolly Green Classroom); pp. 82–83— © Tony Freeman/Photo
Edit (diverse classmates); © Bettmann/Corbis (football players); David J. & Janice L. Frent
Collection/Corbis (busing pin); © Bettmann/Corbis (girls on bus, police escort); p. 84—
San Francisco Chronicle, a division of Hearst Communications, Inc.; SNACK concert poster
designed by Randy Tuten and used with permission.

Cataloging-in-Publication Data available from Library of Congress

IN MEMORY OF
JOHN AND MARY LOUISE MCDONALD

TABLE OF CONTENTS

JULIE'S FAMILY AND FRIENDS

Julie
*A girl full of energy
and new ideas, trying to
find her place in
times of change*

Tracy
*Julie's trendy
teenage sister, who is
fifteen years old*

Mom
*Julie's artistic
mother, who runs
a small store*

Dad
*Julie's father,
an airline pilot who flies
all over the world*

IVY
*Julie's best friend,
who loves doing
gymnastics*

T.J.
*A boy at school
who plays basketball
with Julie*

COACH MANLEY
*A gym teacher
who coaches the
basketball team*

HOMEWORK!

Homework. Julie Albright had never had
so much homework before! At her old
school, all she'd had to do for homework
was fun stuff, like reading *Charlotte's Web* or doing a
word search. But Ms. Hunter's fourth-grade class at
Jack London Elementary had book reports to write,
vocabulary words to memorize, and geography
maps to draw. Julie thought she just might go cross-
eyed staring at the web of pink, green, and yellow
countries and continents.

And now, Ms. Hunter had just announced a new
assignment—a "family project" that would stretch
out over several weeks. Julie winced. Families were
not Julie's favorite topic right now—not since *her*

family had gotten divorced, and Julie, her mother, and her sister had moved to a new neighborhood without Dad.

Julie studied Ms. Hunter's precise penmanship on the blackboard, trying to imitate her teacher's loopy cursive writing as she copied the topic into her own notebook:

The Story of My Life

Just then, Julie's friend T. J. slid a note over to her. Opening it in her lap, she sneaked a peek at it.

The Story of My Life is too much homework!

Julie looked at T. J. and grinned. Then she turned her attention back to her notebook and carefully copied the complete homework assignment from the blackboard:

> *My First Memory*
> *My Brothers and Sisters*
> *When My Mom Was My Age*
> *When My Dad Was My Age*
> *The Best Thing That Ever Happened to Me*
> *The Worst Thing That Ever Happened to Me*

Julie's first memory, when she was three or four, was sneaking into her parents' room and jumping on the big bed when nobody was looking. The Best Thing That Ever Happened was easy—getting to play on the boys' basketball team. It was the Worst Thing that Julie could not imagine writing about. Julie didn't even like *thinking* about her parents' divorce.

"Class," Ms. Hunter was saying, "this project is not just for sitting at your desk and telling me what you remember. I would like each of you to be reporters here. Interview your family members and find out about them. Ask them questions. Learn something new about the people closest to you.

"I want at least one page on each of the topics," Ms. Hunter went on. "You'll also give an oral report to the class about all you've learned."

An oral report to the class! This assignment just kept getting worse. It was bad enough that Julie's parents were divorced, but did she have to tell the whole class about it?

Julie decided she would have to come down with a bad case of The Dog Ate My Homework. Or in her case, The Rabbit Ate My Homework. Maybe she'd come down with writer's cramp. Or writer's block, whatever that was. Julie pictured a gigantic toy block sitting on top of her hand, weighing it down so that she couldn't write.

When Julie went to her locker at the end of the day to grab her gym bag and head for basketball practice, she heard some of her classmates buzzing about their projects. Sure enough, it was the Water Fountain Girls, who loved to chatter and gossip.

"Oh, I can't wait to work on my family project," said Alison. "The best thing ever in my family was when we all went together on a vacation last summer to the Grand Canyon."

"I'm going to tell how my mom and dad went scuba diving for their tenth anniversary and brought back a real shark's tooth for me and my brothers," said Angela.

"My mom's an identical twin, so when my mom and dad were getting married, they played a trick on him and my dad almost married my aunt!" said Amanda. "We still tease him about how my aunt was almost my mom. I could tell that story."

Julie sighed. It was so easy for them. They all

had regular families and happy, funny stories.

Maybe she could make up a pretend story about the Worst Thing That Ever Happened to her. Then she wouldn't have to write about the divorce for the whole entire class. But that would be cheating.

"Earth to Julie," T. J. said, waving his hand in front of her frowning face. "Ready for practice?"

"I was just thinking," said Julie. "About our family report."

"Don't remind me," said T. J. "What are you going to write for the Best Thing Ever?"

"Easy," said Julie. "Getting to play on the basketball team. Being one of the Jaguars is definitely the Best Thing That Ever Happened to Me."

"Speaking of basketball, you know how Coach Manley gets if we're late for practice," said T. J. "We'd better hurry, or we'll both be writing about getting kicked *off* the team for the Worst Thing That Ever Happened."

That afternoon, Dad picked Julie up after school and drove her to his house for the weekend. Funny how she thought of the house she grew up in as

Dad's house now, Julie reflected. As they drove, Julie decided to practice for her assignment. The three best things about staying at Dad's were:

1. Shooting hoops with Dad
2. Seeing Ivy, her best friend, who lived across the street
3. Playing with Nutmeg, her pet rabbit

The three worst things about staying at Dad's were:

1. Missing Mom
2. Missing Tracy (who usually refused to come to Dad's for the weekend)
3. Most of her stuff was at Mom's house now.

When they arrived at Dad's, Julie headed for the back door. "I'm going to get Nutmeg."

"I already brought her in," said Dad. "She's upstairs in your room."

"Thanks, Dad," said Julie, racing up the stairs two at a time. She burst into her old bedroom and was surprised, as always, by how different it looked from before. No rolltop desk, no bookcase, no beanbag chair. The faded flower wallpaper had bright, unfaded rectangles where her posters used to be. This room, these four walls, this shaggy carpet were all she'd known for nine years—her whole life.

But nothing felt familiar anymore. When she called softly to Nutmeg, her voice seemed to echo, bouncing back to her off the blank walls. Julie scooped up Nutmeg from her basket in the corner where the desk used to be and ran back downstairs, keeping ahead of the empty feeling that the room gave her now.

While Dad peeled an apple, Julie perched on the edge of the kitchen counter and dangled an apple peeling in front of Nutmeg's sniffing nose. Nutmeg's whiskers twitched and quivered with excitement.

"You're awfully quiet this afternoon," Dad said.

"Everything okay at school? How's basketball going?"

Julie hesitated. She didn't want to tell Dad how the boys on the other teams sometimes called her mean names just because she was a girl. Instead, she told him about the three steals she'd made in the last game.

"Oh, man. I wish I'd been there," said Dad.

"We have a big game in two weeks, against the Wildcats, and I'm kind of nervous about it," Julie told him. "You're coming, right?"

"You bet I'll be there," said Dad.

"I also have a gigantic school project I have to start working on," Julie sighed.

"You don't sound very happy about it," said Dad.

"It's just that, well . . ." She didn't quite know how to explain to Dad why it was hard for her to write about her family. She didn't want to make him feel bad. "It's just that—my teacher gives so much homework," Julie said finally. She described the Story-of-My-Life project and how she was supposed to interview everyone in her family.

"Sounds like fun to me," Dad said. "I think the

story of Julie Albright will make a great report. You can tell about the time you tried to eat a banana slug, because you thought it was a banana."

"Da-ad! That's way too embarrassing!"

"You were only two," Dad said. "I think it's kind of cute. And funny."

"How about if I write about the time my dad fell into the duck pond at Golden Gate Park when we were playing catch?"

"Okay, okay. Truce!" Dad held up both hands palms out, as if to say *stop*.

"But I do need to interview you, okay, Dad?" Julie picked up a ketchup bottle and spoke into it. "Reporting to you live from the home of Daniel Albright, world-famous pilot. He has just returned from a daring adventure—"

"Hey, wait a second," said Dad. "Hold it right there, Ace. I have an idea." He disappeared into the back room and came out holding both hands behind his back.

"What is it?" asked Julie.

"Something I got for you in Japan. I was planning to put it away for Christmas, but it seems to me you could really use it for your school project.

On the other hand, maybe we should wait," Dad teased.

"Dad! I think it's a great idea to give it to me *now!*" Julie leaped up and faked right, then left, using her fancy footwork from basketball to try to grab whatever Dad was holding behind his back.

"Time out! Foul!" Dad called, blocking Julie. "Okay, okay. I give up." Dad brought his hands out from behind his back, presenting the box he'd been hiding.

"What is it—a transistor radio?" asked Julie, looking at the picture on the front of the box. All the writing was in Japanese.

"It's a portable tape recorder," said Dad. "With a microphone and everything. It'll be great for your interviews, don't you think?" Dad  pointed to the buttons. "See, if you plug in the microphone here, and put in a blank tape, you can use it to record people."

"You mean I can talk and sing into it and stuff?" asked Julie. "Then play it back and hear myself on tape?"

"Yup," said Dad.

"This is so boss! Thank you, Dad," Julie said, hugging him. "Can I go over to Ivy's and show her my new tape recorder?"

"Be back by dinner!" Dad called. Julie was already halfway out the door.

❀

"Hey, Poison Ivy!" Julie said, bursting through the door as soon as her friend opened it.

"Alley Oopster! Or should I call you Alley Hoopster?" said Ivy.

"Look what my dad just gave me. A tape recorder!" Julie held it up.

"Far out," said Ivy, imitating teenagers they heard on TV. "Let's go to my room and try it." Ivy was sucking a grape Popsicle, and she expertly caught a juicy purple drip before it ran down her arm.

"Ooo, keep slurping your Popsicle real loud and I'll tape it." Julie turned on the tape recorder and said, "Testing, testing, one, two, three, testing," into the microphone. Then she held it up to Ivy.

Slurp, slurp. Ivy exaggerated the slurpy-lurpy sounds.

"Louder," Julie prompted. "Now let's rewind

and see if it worked." Julie played back the tape, and the two girls collapsed onto Ivy's bed, laughing.

"Is that what I sound like?" asked Julie. "My voice sounds so weird!"

"Well, don't feel bad. I sounded like a garbage disposal," said Ivy, prompting even more giggles.

"What else can we tape?" Julie asked. The girls wandered around Ivy's house, taping anything they discovered that made a noise. They taped Ivy's little sister, Missy, crying for one more cookie. They taped Ivy's brother, Andrew, snoring while he napped on the sofa. They taped Ivy's mother singing to herself in Chinese while she stirred a pot of soup on the stove.

When they played the tape back, Julie said, "Your little sister's so cute, even when she's crying."

"Yeah, but you don't get stuck babysitting her," said Ivy.

"I wish I did," said Julie. "I can't wait till I'm old enough to babysit."

"Hey, I know—let's make some sound effects," said Ivy. "Like they do in plays and movies."

"Great idea," said Julie. Putting pairs of wooden-soled clogs onto their hands, the girls clip-clopped against the floor to

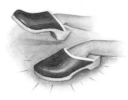

sound like a giant tromping down the stairs. A squeaky door sounded like a mouse when Julie held the microphone up to its hinges. For rain, they turned on the shower.

"The toilet!" said Julie. "Pretend you're about to get flushed down the toilet."

"Help!" cried Ivy. "Save me! A giant whirlpool is about to—"*Ker-plushhh!* Ivy flushed the toilet while Julie held out the microphone. They bit their lips to keep from laughing.

"Let's hear it," said Julie, hitting the rewind button. They listened to their entire collection of sound effects. When it came to the flushing toilet, Ivy said, "That sounds like Yosemite Falls!" They played it over and over, laughing harder each time.

"Hey, Ivy, I gotta go," Julie said finally. "Dad said to be home by dinnertime."

"See you later," said Ivy. "And don't forget to blink your lights tonight when you go to bed, and I'll blink mine."

It was their secret good-night code. "I won't forget," Julie told her friend.

with all the fun she'd had over the weekend. But when she turned to wave good-bye to Dad, she couldn't help but feel a now-familiar pang, knowing Dad was headed back, by himself, to the too-quiet house full of empty rooms.

Julie watched the beams of Dad's headlights fade as his car disappeared down the hill, and she headed inside and into the kitchen, where heavenly smells coaxed away her sad feelings.

"Hi, honey," said Mom. "How was your weekend?"

"Good. Mom, what's that great smell?"

"Just meat loaf in the oven," said Mom. "And I made gravy for the potatoes."

"It smells yummy, Mom. Hey, look what Dad brought me from Japan." Julie pulled out her tape recorder, pushed the record button, and held up the microphone.

"We're here above the famous shop Gladrags, speaking with owner Joyce Albright. Mrs. Albright, who is normally hard at work running her store, is today making a rare appearance in the kitchen. Tell us, Mrs. Albright, what's cooking for dinner?"

"I already told you it's meat loaf," said Mom.

"Well, then, what is it you're making now that's getting flour all over your apron?"

Mom dusted off her hands and brushed her apron, puffing a small cloud of fine flour in the air. "Cherry pie. All this flour is from rolling out the crust."

"Like Grandma's?" Julie asked, momentarily forgetting her reporter role. "With the fancy crust and vanilla ice cream on top?"

"That's the one," said Mom. "Julie, honey, could you put that microphone down and start setting the table? We'll be ready to eat in about ten minutes, as soon as this goes into the oven."

"Where's Tracy? It's her turn to set the table."

"Then get your sister," said Mom.

Julie set down her tape recorder, but as she started down the hall, Tracy pushed past her into the kitchen. "Mom says come set the table," Julie told her sister.

"It's not my turn to set the table," said Tracy, plucking a carrot from the salad as Mom pretend-swatted her hand.

"You're cracked. I set the table last, on Thursday, 'cause the next day I left for Dad's," Julie retorted.

17

"Well, I set it for the last *two* nights in a row, while you were gone," said Tracy.

"Yeah, well, so did I, at Dad's. That's *three* nights in a row for me. But what would you know? You didn't even come to Dad's."

"Girls, girls!" said Mom. "Enough with the Hundred Years' War. Julie hasn't even been back ten minutes and you two are already at it. Tracy, get the plates and glasses. Julie, set out the silverware. You haven't seen each other all weekend, and I want us to have a nice, peaceful dinner together."

"Well, she started it," said Julie.

Mom gave Julie a sharp look. "I don't want to have to tell you again. If you two don't stop bickering, there will be no cherry pie for dessert."

"What? You made cherry pie?" asked Tracy.

"Just like Grandma's," said Julie. "With ladders for the crust and everything."

"*Lattice*," said Mom.

"Yum!" said Julie.

"That's one thing we can agree on!" Tracy grinned.

MEET CHARLOTTE

 The next day after school, the string of brass bells jingled as Julie came in through the front door of Gladrags, calling, "Hello? Anybody home?" She made her way past racks of ponchos and peasant shirts, Mexican masks and blankets, and shelves of sandalwood incense.

"Hi, honey," Mom called from the back room. "Good timing. I was just fixing myself a cup of tea. How was school today?"

"Fine, Mom. Is now a good time to tape you?"

"Sure, but if any customers come—"

Julie was already dashing upstairs. She grabbed her tape recorder and hurried back down to the shop.

Julie held out the microphone, and Mom began telling her all about the time when she was ten, growing up on an apple farm in Santa Rosa, north of San Francisco.

"I got a horse named Firefly for my tenth birthday, and of course I couldn't wait to ride her. I'd begged and pleaded for a whole year, wanting a horse of my own. But before I even climbed into the saddle, the horse got spooked and acted all crazy, rearing and jumping and bucking."

"Whoa," Julie whispered.

"She broke away from your grandpa, who was holding the reins, and ran out through the garden and around the apple orchard. We chased her for half the morning. Finally she stepped on her reins, and that stopped her."

"What spooked her so badly?" asked Julie.

"Later we discovered poor Firefly had been stung by a bee right on her nose. So I finally got my horse, but after that incident, I was afraid to ride her for the longest time."

Just as Mom was finishing her story, Tracy came in and plunked a towering armload of schoolbooks on the table. "Shh!" Julie mouthed, holding a finger

"What spooked her so badly?" asked Julie.

the extra privacy she needed to listen to her secret tape. She switched on the closet light, hit rewind, and adjusted the volume to low.

At first, Tracy's talk with her friend Suzanne was just boring stuff about kids Julie didn't know, such as which girls liked which boys and what to wear to some dance. Then, halfway into the conversation, Julie couldn't believe her ears. She hit rewind and played it again.

A secret like this was too big to hold in. A secret like this—especially when it was about your big sister—was meant to be shared.

Julie peeked out of her bedroom door. The coast was clear. She ran to the kitchen and dialed Ivy's number, stretching the cord all the way to her room this time, ignoring the warning she'd given Tracy a little while ago.

"Hey, Ivy. It's me. Want to hear a super-duper juicy secret?"

"Sure! That's what friends are for, isn't it?"

Both girls giggled nervously. "It's not about me," Julie explained. "It's about Tracy. I got it on tape. Listen to this. But you have to promise you won't tell. Cross your heart?"

"Of course I won't tell! What is it?"

Julie pushed the play button and held the phone receiver up to the tape recorder.

Suzanne: When did this happen?

Tracy: At the movies last Saturday. I went to see *Jaws* with a bunch of kids from the tennis team, but I like this one boy, Matt, so I made Jill switch seats so I could sit next to him.

Suzanne: What did Matt do?

Tracy: Well, first I thought he didn't even like me. But he did share his SweetTarts with me. Then, the next thing I knew, there's this long part where they're on the boat, and it's real quiet, and...

Suzanne: Yeah, yeah, what happened?

Tracy: He reached over and held my hand, just like that. I was so surprised I almost swallowed my gum.

Suzanne: (squealing) He held your hand?

Tracy: Yeah! I thought everything was going great, but then, right after the movie, he told me I chewed my gum too loud during the scary parts.

Suzanne: He said that? Rude!

Julie hit stop. "Ivy, could you hear all that? My sister has a boyfriend! Tracy and Matt, sitting in a tree," Julie chanted.

"Yuck, I can't believe she really likes a boy."

"Yep, and I know who he is, too. I've seen him at Tracy's tennis matches. He has really blond hair and peach fuzz on his lip that looks like a milk mustache."

"Gross!" said Ivy. "Are you going to tell her you know?"

"Well, if I do, she'll ask how I found out. She'd never believe it was just by chance. Still, it would be a waste not to bug her about it *some*how!"

I wanna hold your hand,
I wanna hold your ha-a-a-and!
I wanna hold your hand.

Julie was singing a Beatles song into her microphone and dancing around her room after dinner when Tracy poked her head in the doorway.

"Knock-knock," said Tracy. "I hate to interrupt the concert, but Mom says she could really use our help downstairs in the shop. She got a whole shipment of night-lights today."

"I'll help," said Julie, dropping her microphone on the bed. She pushed past Tracy and headed down the back steps. "Last one there's a rotten egg,"she shouted as she raced down the stairs ahead of Tracy.

Mom set two big boxes on the back worktable. "Girls, can you unpack these night-lights? Be careful with the seashells. We have to put them together first, then price each one."

Julie lifted some delicate shells out of the box. "Wow, look at this shell," she said, holding up a round purplish globe. "It almost looks like a starfish on top."

"That's a sea urchin," said Mom. "It works like a mini lampshade." Mom showed them how to assemble one of the night-lights, carefully placing the globe over a small night-light bulb and then plugging it in to make sure it worked.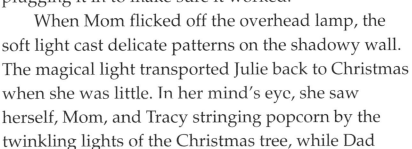

When Mom flicked off the overhead lamp, the soft light cast delicate patterns on the shadowy wall. The magical light transported Julie back to Christmas when she was little. In her mind's eye, she saw herself, Mom, and Tracy stringing popcorn by the twinkling lights of the Christmas tree, while Dad stood on a stepladder pinning the star to the very top of the tree.

"I want one of these for my room," said Tracy, breaking the spell.

"I can make you a really good deal," said Mom, chuckling.

The girls set to work assembling the night-lights and putting price stickers on the bottom of each one. Julie loved handling the pretty seashells and trying to decide which shape she liked best. She felt like an elf in Santa's workshop. What fun it was, to be helping Mom in the back of the shop after hours! It occurred to her that if her parents hadn't split up, her mother might never have opened Gladrags. Julie sighed, confused. How could she feel so torn between the way things used to be and the way her life was now?

Tracy pulled a conch shell out of the box. All of a sudden, she put one hand up to her forehead, making a fin, and sang, "*Dun-dun! Dun-dun, dun-dun!*" in a deep, ominous, hollow-drum-sounding voice.

Julie tilted her head, looking puzzled.

"It's the music from the movie *Jaws*," Tracy

explained. "You know, the great white shark. Don't go in the water," she warned in a creepy voice, then reached out to grab Julie's leg.

"Aaah!" screamed Julie, almost dropping one of the fragile shells.

"Girls, be careful. These break easily," Mom cautioned.

"So, you liked the movie?" Julie casually asked.

"Yeah. I'm going to go see it again," said Tracy.

"I didn't think *Jaws* was still playing in theaters," Mom said.

"There's this one theater in San Francisco that still plays it all the time," said Tracy. "And everybody screams when the shark attacks, no matter how many times they've seen it." Tracy turned back to the night-lights. "They made a giant model of a shark for the movie," she added. "It's called Bruce."

"How do you know that?" asked Julie.

"My friend told me. He got the poster with a picture of it at the theater," said Tracy.

"*He?*" asked Julie. "As in *boy*friend?"

"Grow up," said Tracy. "When you're in high school, you can have friends that are boys. It's no big deal."

Tracy was always acting so superior! Well, for once Tracy wasn't the only one with special, *insider* knowledge.

"Did you get anything to eat at the movies?" Julie asked.

"Not really," said Tracy.

"Not even gum?" Julie pressed.

"Huh? What are you talking about?"

"Oh, I was just thinking about how it's fun to chew gum at the movies—like during the scary parts, it helps to not be scared if you chew your gum *real loud.*"

Tracy opened her eyes wide and shot Julie a look. A how-do-you-know-that, you'd-better-not-say-another-word look. Julie could see the machinery of Tracy's mind turning it over like a tricky math problem as she struggled to figure out how Julie knew about the gum.

"My, you girls sure are quiet all of a sudden," Mom remarked.

"Mom, how much longer do you think this will take? I have homework," said Tracy. "Julie does, too, don't you?" Tracy challenged her younger sister with her eyes.

"Go on up," said Mom. "You girls were really a big help tonight. Thank you."

The second they got to the top of the stairs, Tracy turned on Julie, wagging an accusing finger at her. "You eavesdropped on me! You listened right outside my door when I was on the phone with Suzanne, didn't you? Admit it."

"I did not. I was nowhere near your room when you were on the phone. I was right here almost the whole time," said Julie, walking into her room and pointing to her bed.

Tracy followed her. "What was all that about the gum, then?"

"I have homework, remember?" said Julie, plopping down on her bed.

"I'm not leaving till you tell me what you heard."

"How's Matt the gnat?" Julie teased.

"Oh!" Tracy huffed, hands on her hips. "You, you—" she stuttered, but words wouldn't come out.

"Tra-cy has a boy-friend," Julie teased in a sing-song voice.

"I do not! You better not tell anybody!"

"Do too! I have proof, right here." Julie popped

out the cassette tape and held it up, taunting her sister.

"Who do you think you are, Little Miss Watergate? Give me that tape," said Tracy, reaching over and snatching it out of Julie's hand.

"Hey, that's my homework. Give it back!"

Tracy held the tape out of Julie's reach. "Don't you know it's illegal to tape someone without telling them?"

It was? Julie felt a twinge of guilt, but she mustered a comeback anyway. "So, what are you going to do, call the police?"

Tracy hesitated, glaring at her sister, then tossed the tape on the floor. Julie snatched it up.

"You better not tell anyone about this!" Tracy hissed through clenched teeth. "I mean it, Julie." She stomped out of the room, and Julie heard the angry slam of Tracy's door down the hall.

Just then, Mom came into Julie's room with a startled look. "What was that all about?"

"Nothing," said Julie. "Mom, what's Watergate?"

"A few years ago, President Nixon hired people to spy on his political opponents. When he got caught, he lied and tried to cover it up. But some secret tapes revealed that he was lying, so he resigned from being president. That's why Gerald Ford is our president now." Mom raised her eyebrows. "Why do you ask?"

"Tracy just called me Little Miss Watergate. But I wasn't lying about anything," Julie said innocently. "I was just trying to tape her for my project."

Mom gave Julie a serious look. "It's okay for your school project," she said, "*if* you have her permission. But otherwise, I don't want you bothering your sister with that tape recorder. "

CHAPTER

THREE

—

THIS LITTLE PIGGY

At school the next day, Ms. Hunter took the class to the library to read biographies. Julie chose a biography of Clara Barton and sat down next to T. J.

"What'd you get?" she whispered. He held up a book about Daniel Boone.

Julie looked down at her book and tried to concentrate on the words she was reading: "Clara Barton, angel of the Civil War battlefield, watched over her patients as the surgeon dressed their wounds with cornhusks."

She tried not to look at T. J. One look at her friend and she knew she'd start giggling. But finally she turned to T. J. again.

"Are you going to be at practice today after school?" she whispered.

"Of course. It's only two weeks to the big game."

"Yikes! Two weeks till we play the Wildcats," Julie whispered.

"They're undefeated," said T. J. "And they have this one player—"

"Class," said Ms. Hunter, "remember what I said about visiting with your neighbor. This is supposed to be silent reading."

After basketball practice, Coach Manley called the team into a huddle. "Johnson, work on that defense inside the key. Albright, I've seen notes in class passed faster than your bounce pass. McDermott, what's with all the fouls? Tomorrow you'd better be over your case of the clumsies. That's it, players. See you tomorrow."

As soon as Coach Manley was out of earshot, T. J. muttered, "What got into Coach today? I feel like I just ran a marathon or something."

"What's wrong with my defense, anyway?" complained Paul Johnson, point guard for the Jaguars.

"And I had one of my best passes ever," Julie chimed in. "I think Coach Manley needs glasses."

"He's just uptight about playing the Wildcats. He thinks we're not ready to take them on," said Tommy McDermott, the team captain.

"At this rate, we're going to be too *tired* to play the Wildcats," said T. J., and everybody laughed.

"I hear they have this one fifth grader who's practically six feet tall," said Tony Monteverdi, who played center. "They call him Dunk because he can jam balls right through the hoop."

"Yeah, he thinks he's the next Kareem Abdul-Jabbar," said Brian Hannigan, the team's forward. Brian was five foot eight himself, but even he looked worried.

"Great," said Julie. "I bet he's just going to love playing against a team with a girl."

"Hey, don't go thinking that way," said Paul. "You're one of the best ball handlers we've got on this team. We don't call you Cool Hand Albright for nothing."

Kareem Abdul-Jabbar

"Really? You guys gave me a nickname?"

"Are you kidding?" said T. J. "You can dribble rings around half this team."

38

All the way home, Julie couldn't stop thinking about the Wildcats. Just the thought of going up against the legendary Dunk made her shiver. To chase away the goose bumps, Julie recalled Paul's words. *One of the best ball handlers.* She could still feel the warm glow of the compliment.

Cool Hand Albright. Her very own nickname!

On Saturday morning, Julie set up an obstacle course on the sidewalk with a laundry basket, an empty scrub bucket, and a family-sized box of detergent. She weaved her way in and out of the obstacles, switching hands, practicing her dribbling, then pretending to palm off the ball in a bounce pass to an imaginary player.

"Hey! Whatya doing?" a voice asked. Tracy.

"Practicing my bounce pass. Coach Manley told me it needs work."

"Well, it looks pretty good to me," said Tracy cheerfully. "Want me to stand in? You can go through the course, then pass the ball off to me."

"Hey, wait a minute," said Julie. "I thought you weren't talking to me. Now you're trying to help me with basketball? What's up?"

"Nothing," said Tracy. "I'm over it. Besides, I can't stay mad at my little sister forever, can I?" She leaned in and gave Julie a sideways hug.

"I'm not doing the dishes for you tonight, if that's what you're thinking," Julie replied.

"No, of course not," said Tracy. "C'mon, why don't you start dribbling, then pass the ball to me."

"Well, okay, thanks. Ready?" asked Julie.

For the next several minutes, Julie weaved, turned, faked, and drove the ball this way and that, bounce-passing it to Tracy, who passed it right back. In the scramble, Tracy kicked over the bucket and Julie knocked into the detergent, spilling white powder all over the sidewalk. Between bounce passes, Tracy tried to steal the ball, but Julie was too fast.

"Time out!" Tracy called, winded. The two girls gulped in air and sat down on a nearby front step.

"By the way," Tracy said, absentmindedly curling a strand of hair around her finger, "you know how you've been dying to baby-sit?"

"Yeah, but Mom says I'm still too young," Julie replied. "Why? You know somebody who needs a babysitter?"

Tracy tried to steal the ball, but Julie was too fast.

"Umm—sort of."

"Who?" Julie bolted upright, excited by the possibility of her first job. "When can I start? Do you think Mom'll let me? How much do they pay?"

"Well, since it's your first time, it would have to be for free. You know, to get experience. Then you work up to the big bucks."

"I don't know," said Julie, leaning back on her elbows. "On *The Brady Bunch*, Marcia and Greg get their parents to pay them just to babysit their own brothers and sisters."

"Well, this isn't *The Brady Bunch*," said Tracy. "Could you start later today?"

"You mean it? For real? How old is the kid? What's the kid's name?"

Tracy hesitated. She glanced sideways at Julie. "Charlotte?" she said, making it sound like a question.

"It's your plant!" Julie said in disbelief. "You want me to babysit a dumb old plant? That's why you're being all nice and helping me with basketball and everything?"

"C'mon, Jules, you'd really be helping me out. It's super easy—you'd hardly have to do anything.

Just go in my room and check on it a couple times while I'm gone. If the soil feels dry, give it a little water. And if you notice anything different or unusual, just write it down so that I can record it in my science journal."

"I can't. Ivy's coming for a sleepover, and I might forget. Besides, what's so important that you can't do it yourself? You're probably just hanging out with your friends at the Doggy Diner."

"Not this time," said Tracy. She lowered her voice to a conspiratorial whisper. "See, I'm going to my friend Jill's house with a bunch of people, and her brother has a VW bug. Have you ever heard of Volkswagen stuffing? We're going to see how many kids we can pile into one little VW bug. It's like playing Twister times ten."

"That sounds weird," said Julie.

"It's going to be crazy fun," said Tracy, "and Jill invited me to spend the night at her house. I really want to go, but I'll get points marked off if I skip two whole days in my journal."

"I never heard of such a dopey idea—baby-sitting a plant."

"Sure, it's called plant-sitting. You can make a lot

of money taking care of people's houseplants when they go away."

"Really? Plant-sitting, huh? Okay, I'll do it. But it'll cost you. Two dollars."

"Two dollars! Are you nuts? For maybe watering it once and making sure it doesn't croak?"

"Take it or leave it," said Julie, crossing her arms to show that her mind was made up.

"One dollar," said Tracy.

"Deal," said Julie.

"The eensy-weensy spider went up the water spout," Julie sang to the plant on her bedroom windowsill. Ivy joined in, adding all the hand motions that went with the song.

"Tell me again why we're singing to a plant?" Ivy asked.

"It's for Tracy's science project. She asked me to watch her plant this weekend, but I was afraid I'd forget, so I just brought it in here. There's more sunlight in my room, anyway," said Julie. "And I read in a magazine that if you sing to plants or play music around them, they grow faster."

"Really? That sounds wacky," said Ivy.

"I know," Julie admitted. "But wouldn't it be great if Tracy came back and her plant had grown a whole inch? She'd get extra credit for sure. Let's sing it again!"

"Okay, once last time," Ivy agreed. "Then let's go do something outside."

"I know—this time I'll tape us singing!" said Julie. "Then I can just play the tape for Charlotte."

When the girls were finished singing, Julie pressed the play button and then picked up her basketball. "Want to go shoot some hoops?"

"Sure," said Ivy. "Let me get my shoes on."

"Think fast!" Julie said, tossing a pass to Ivy. But Ivy had bent down to pull on her boots. The ball hit the dresser, rattling Julie's gumball machine, then zinged off the corner, heading right for the open window.

"Noooooo!" Julie dove across the bed, lunging to save the ball from going out the window. The basketball thumped against the windowsill, then bounced into Julie's hands. "Whew—got it!"

Ivy stared at the window in horror.

Crash.

"What was that?" Julie followed Ivy's gaze to the open window—and empty windowsill.

For a split second, Julie's mouth gaped open in shock. Then Julie and Ivy rushed over to the window and peered down at the sidewalk below. Charlotte lay in a jumbled heap on the ground. Dirt was scattered all over the sidewalk. The clay hippo was smashed to pieces.

In a blur, Julie and Ivy raced down the back steps and out onto the sidewalk.

"Oh, no!" said Julie, covering her face in disbelief. "What are we going to do?" She picked up the spider plant, turning it in her hand. Many of the long, blade-like leaves were crushed and broken, and the roots looked pale and limp.

"Maybe the roots are still okay," Ivy said hopefully. "And we can clean up all this dirt. It's probably still perfectly good dirt."

"But the pot—we've got to put it back together."

Ivy shook her head. "There are too many pieces. We'll never be able to glue it."

"Then we'll have to find another pot just like it," said Julie, picking up the pieces.

"Does your mom have more pots like this

at her shop?" Ivy asked.

"No, that's the problem. This one was just a sample," Julie explained.

"I've seen them at the Five-and-Ten Shop in Chinatown," said Ivy. "My mom has one that's a frog."

"Hey, there's a Five-and-Ten Shop right down on Haight Street," said Julie, brushing the last of the dirt off the sidewalk. "I'll go get a bag to carry Charlotte in and tell my mom we're going. Come on!"

On Haight Street, the girls rushed past the bead shop, the record store, and the art-supply store. At the antique store, Ivy paused to admire a silk kimono on a mannequin in the window, while Julie peeked at Charlotte, who lay in a soft bag that was made from an old pair of blue jeans. Charlotte looked a bit crushed.

"Mom's told me a million times not to throw the basketball in the house. Now I know why," Julie murmured. "Come on, we better hurry."

At the Five-and-Ten Shop, Ivy followed Julie past a pyramid of Charlie perfume and down an aisle filled with old Halloween candy.

"There's the plant section," Julie said, motioning to Ivy. They walked past rows of African violets and begonias, looking for the pots.

Ivy paused to admire a silk kimono on a mannequin in the window.

48

"Over there!" said Ivy. "I see one that's a turtle." They scanned the cluttered shelf, searching for a planter in the shape of a hippo, like Tracy's.

"They have bunnies and puppies, cows and kittens," said Julie. "There just has to be a hippo." She began lifting out all the pots stacked behind the front row and setting them on the floor.

"May I help you?" asked a tall woman wearing a blue smock with a name tag that said "Glenda." She peered at them over glasses attached to a chain around her neck.

"Sorry," said Julie. "We'll put these all back. We're just looking for a hippo."

"It's an emergency," Ivy explained.

"The puppies are very cute," said Glenda. "They're our most popular item."

Both girls shook their heads. "It has to be a hippo."

"I don't think we've ever carried a hippo, but we might be able to order one," Glenda offered.

"You don't understand," said Julie. "This is my sister's plant, for a school project. She had it in a hippo planter, and I broke it!"

"Oh, I think I'm getting the picture. Tell you what. We have a few piggies left, over here," Glenda said, lifting one down from a high-up shelf. "Don't you think it looks a bit like a hippo?"

Julie looked at Ivy. Ivy shrugged. "It's pretty close," she told her friend.

"We could even call it Wilbur, like the pig in *Charlotte's Web*. But not to Tracy, of course," said Julie. She turned to Glenda. "Okay, we'll take it."

"Would you like me to pot it up for you?" Glenda asked, glancing at the limp plant in Julie's hand. "I can trim off some of those broken leaves."

"Really? That'd be great. Does it cost extra?"

"Not for emergencies." Glenda winked at Julie. "I'll have to take it in the back. Why don't you girls look around and come back in fifteen minutes?"

While they waited, Julie and Ivy wandered over to the pet section. They tried to get the parakeets to talk, watched two hamsters run a race on their wheels, and gazed at the hermit crabs, hoping to catch one changing shells. At the turtle tank, they made up names for some of the baby turtles, like Slow Poke and Cutie

hermit crab

Pie. One turtle had gotten stuck on its back, so the girls reached in and helped it to flip over.

"Julie and Ivy to the rescue!" said Ivy.

"It's probably been fifteen minutes," said Julie. "Let's go see if Wilbur and Charlotte are ready."

At the counter, Glenda handed them the spider plant. "Well, I can't say it's good as new, but it should pull through. Be sure to give it a good drink when you get home."

"Thanks a million!" said Julie as she paid for the pot. "It looks better already."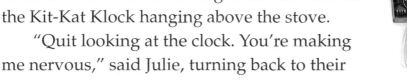

"And the leaves cover up the pot, so you can't really tell it's not a hippo," said Ivy.

"Be careful now," said Glenda, waving. "You don't want to make any more trips to the plant hospital today."

The girls smiled and waved good-bye as they headed out the door. "Time for this little piggy to go home!" said Julie.

The next afternoon, Julie and Ivy sat with their legs folded under them at the kitchen table, riveted to the tick-tick-ticking of the cat's tail on the Kit-Kat Klock hanging above the stove.

"Quit looking at the clock. You're making me nervous," said Julie, turning back to their game of Chinese checkers.

"The way the cat's eyeballs move back and forth, I feel like he's staring at me," said Ivy, jumping a marble twice. "Do you think Tracy's going to know something happened to her plant?"

"I hope not. Because if that plant dies, she might flunk her assignment."

"Uh-oh," said Ivy.

"Speaking of assignments, one *good* thing about all this is I have a new idea for my report. Best Thing Ever: my first paid plant-sitting job. Worst Thing Ever: knocking Charlotte out the window." Julie moved a marble into her home triangle. "Remember, when Tracy gets here, just act natural."

"Don't worry," said Ivy. "She'll be so busy thinking about dreamboat Matt, she probably won't even notice."

Five minutes later, the front door opened, and Tracy called out, "Hey, everybody. I'm ba-ack!"

"Good, sounds like she's in a good mood," Julie whispered to Ivy.

"Anybody home?" Tracy called.

"We're in the kitchen," Julie called back. She swallowed hard and stared at the marbles on the board as her sister entered the room.

"Hi, Ivy," said Tracy.

"So, did you and your friends break any world records?" asked Julie. "You know, for the number of people in a Volkswagen?"

"I think we broke the record for the number of *squished* people," said Tracy. "So, anything happening around here?"

"No!" Julie glanced nervously at Ivy, who was rolling a marble between her fingers. "What makes you say that?"

"Nothing, I was just asking," said Tracy. She picked up her backpack. "Well, I'm going to go change."

"She didn't even ask about Charlotte," Julie whispered when Tracy had left the room.

Suddenly they heard a shriek. Tracy's door flew open and she yelled down the hall, "Julie, what in the world did you do?"

Julie hurried to Tracy's room, with Ivy right behind her. "What do you mean? What's wrong?" she asked.

Tracy pointed at the spider plant on her desk. "My plant looks *smaller*. Like it shrunk. And the tips of the leaves are turning brown! Are you sure you watered it, like I said?" Tracy asked.

"Positive. We held it under the faucet for like five minutes. Didn't we, Ivy?"

Ivy bit her lip and nodded. "Yeah, and we put it in Julie's window so it would get more sunlight. We sang to it, too."

"Great, you probably overwatered it. Plants can drown, you know. And it's not supposed to be in direct sunlight. No wonder the tips are brown!"

"Maybe some music will help," said Julie. "We made Charlotte a tape—want us to play it?"

"Never mind," said Tracy with a heavy sigh. "I'll just have to put these observations in my journal."

Julie and Ivy wandered back to the kitchen table and gazed at the Chinese checkers board.

"I think it's your move," said Julie, but the game no longer seemed fun.

"Hey, she didn't even notice Wilbur," said Ivy.

"Yeah," said Julie. "That's good, at least."

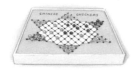

C H A P T E R
F O U R
—

THE BIG GAME

Three more days. Two more days. One more day. Julie deliberately marked a red crayon X through each day leading up to the big game with the Wildcats, the Thursday that had been circled on her calendar for the last three weeks.

All of a sudden, Julie came up with a new idea for her report.

Best Thing Ever: the big game was finally here.

Worst Thing Ever: the big game was really and truly here! *Aaieee!*

She looked in the mirror and took a deep breath, willing herself steady. Uniform? Check. Sneakers? Check. Tube socks? Check. Sweatband? Check. Julie stuffed the items she'd need into her gym bag, double- and triple-checking to make sure she had everything.

"All ready?" asked Mom, poking her head into Julie's room. "I made French toast this morning. Thought you could use a real breakfast for your big day. And I put some granola bars in your lunch in case you need some quick energy after school before the game."

"Thanks, Mom." Julie's voice came out in a tiny squeak.

"Nervous?" asked Mom.

"A little," said Julie. "Excited, too. I just wish you could be there."

"I know, honey. I'm disappointed, too. Of all the days for the bank to schedule a big meeting to talk about my business loan. But Dad'll be there. I'm sure he'll take some pictures. And you can tell me all about it, play by play."

Mom drove Julie to school that morning and gave her an extra-special squeeze before Julie got out of the car. "Remember, take a deep breath, and just do your best. That's all anybody can ask."

"See ya later, Hoopster," said Tracy, sliding out of the front bench seat so Julie could climb out. "Go easy on those boys, now. Don't make those Wildcats look too bad." Julie giggled. "I'll try to be there by the second half, if tennis practice is over," Tracy told her.

"Bye!" Julie waved.

"One, two, three… Go, Jaguars!" Julie, T. J., and the other players broke from the huddle, and the big game was on. The opening jump ball went to the Wildcats, and it was all the Jaguars could do to keep up. Elbows were flying and feet racing, and the crowd was already up out of their seats, cheering as the ball moved up and down the court.

"Defense, defense!" Coach Manley yelled to his players.

Julie double-teamed with T. J. to try to block the tall kid, Wildcat Number 16, also known as Dunk.

"Hey, 22, forget your cheerleading pom-poms?" Dunk snickered as he stole the ball out from under Julie. Then he elbowed right past her, shoving her out of the way. It was the third time he had fouled her, but the ref had only called a foul once.

"Hey, no fair," Julie called.

"That's a foul, 'fraidy-cats!" T. J. shouted.

Julie knew her dad worried about rough playing, and he would not be happy about it. She tried to spot him in the stands, but the game was moving fast and she couldn't find him.

Julie ran downcourt. With a minute left in the first half, the Jaguars were down by six points, but they had the ball.

"Hey, ballerina," called Number 16. "Where's your tutu?"

Julie gritted her teeth. She had to concentrate, focus, do everything Coach Manley had taught them in practice to block out distractions and drive the ball so that her team could score.

Then Dunk was on her again, so she quickly passed the ball to T. J. He was instantly surrounded and had to pass the ball back. Just as the ball reached Julie's hands, Dunk lunged, grasping for the ball and knocking Julie flat on the floor.

The shrill sound of the ref's whistle stopped the game. Julie curled up on the court, holding her hand close to her chest in pain. Next thing she knew, she was being helped off the court, and Tracy was at her side.

"Where's Dad?" Julie asked in a shaky voice.

"You mean he's not here?" Tracy said. "I just got here myself. Are you okay?"

"Let's have a look at that hand," said Coach Manley. He was already calling for ice and a first-aid kit.

"It's my finger. It bent back under me when I was pushed down. I can't move it."

"Yeah, you have some swelling, all right. We'll ice it, and we need to get you to the emergency room and have it looked at," said Coach Manley. "Better get an X-ray to be on the safe side."

"Leave the game? Please, no!" If she left the game now, people would *really* think that girls shouldn't play basketball. "Coach, can't we tape it up or something so that I can stay in? Can I at least make my foul shot?"

"No. I hope it's just a sprain, but I'm not taking any chances," said Coach Manley. "Is your mom or dad here?"

"Just my sister," said Julie.

"Our dad's supposed to be here," said Tracy, "but I don't see him anywhere."

T. J. was standing right next to Julie. "My mom's here. She could take you," he offered, running over to the bleachers to alert his mother.

Tracy helped Julie out through the gym door, and the sounds of the clapping, cheering crowd began to fade as they walked down the empty hall and out the front doors of the school. Clutching her injured finger to her chest, Julie couldn't help thinking that leaving the game hurt almost as much as the pulsing and throbbing of her swollen finger.

Julie sat tense and rigid in a straight-backed chair in the hospital waiting room. Holding ice to her purple, swollen finger, she fought back the tears.

"Are you okay, honey?" T. J.'s mother asked, putting her hand on Julie's shoulder. "Can I get you anything?"

"Just my mom and dad," Julie sniffed, trying to put on a good face. So much for Cool Hand Albright. How could her hand have let her down like this?

"Tracy's calling them now, and by the time you get done with the doctor, I'm sure they'll be here, said T. J.'s mother."

"You don't understand," said Julie. "My mom

and dad don't live together anymore. They're . . .
divorced. My dad was supposed to be at the game,
and I don't know what happened. Tracy already
called Mom twice and can't reach her, either."

"Well, I'll stay with you girls until we reach one
of your parents. Don't you worry about that. Right
now, we just need to get you in to the doctor and
feeling better."

Just then, Tracy came back from using the pay
phone.

"Any luck?" T. J.'s mother asked Tracy.

"Still no answer. Mom had to go to a meeting at
the bank today. She must not be back yet, and I don't
know which bank it is. My dad has a new answering
machine, so I left him a message on it. I guess I'll just
keep trying."

"Julie Albright," called a nurse, looking down at
her clipboard. "Julie Albright."

Julie and Tracy spent nearly an hour behind a
curtain at the emergency room while the doctor took
x-rays of Julie's finger. Then he listened to her heart,
looked into her ears, and shone a bright beam of light

in her eyes. By the time she emerged, her arm was resting safely in a sling, and her broken finger was splinted and taped to its neighbor so that she couldn't bend it or move it.

Julie and Tracy both looked up and down the waiting area, trying to spot T. J.'s mom.

"There she is," a familiar voice exclaimed. Dad! Julie looked up. Rushing down the hall toward her were Mom *and* Dad. Together.

They hurried over to Julie, enfolding her in one big hug. All the tears that she'd been holding back came out in a flood of relief.

"Honey, honey, we just heard. Are you okay?" Mom asked, dabbing tears from Julie's face with the corner of her scarf. "Does it hurt? You girls must have been so scared," she said, looking up at Tracy. "Thank you so much," she added, turning to T. J.'s mother.

"We got here as fast as we could," said Dad, kneeling down to take a closer look at Julie's finger and splint. "What happened? Is anything broken?"

"We were at Julie's basketball game," said Tracy. "This big kid from the other team kept pushing Julie. He wouldn't leave her alone—"

"And they weren't even calling it a foul," added Julie, finding words coming back to her. "Then next thing I knew, he knocked into me, and I fell and landed on my finger. It bent way back the wrong way and hurt really bad and—"

"She broke her finger!" Tracy interrupted, looking back and forth from Mom to Dad.

"Except the doctor kept calling it a *phalange*," said Julie. "Now I'm like a robot," she added, holding up her splinted finger to show off all the metal and gauze around it.

"We'll take care of your finger, and it'll heal soon," Mom reassured her. "I'm just so sorry this happened."

"We're very proud of both of you girls," said Dad. "Tracy, honey, I know this was a lot for you to handle—"

"Where were you, Dad?" Tracy snapped. "Weren't you supposed to be there? What if I hadn't made it to the game after tennis?" Tracy's voice was shaking.

"Tracy," Mom said gently, "your father had a weather delay out of Chicago, and there was nothing he could do. These things happen, and it's nobody's fault. We're all just relieved that Julie's okay."

"I tried to call you a bunch of times," Tracy accused Mom.

"I know," said Mom. "It's a good thing Dad got that answering machine. He got your message and called me right away, and we came here just as soon as we could. You did the right thing, honey. I know how scary it is when you're worried like that." Mom pulled Tracy closer, stroking her hair.

"You came with Dad? Together? In the same car?" Julie asked.

"Yes, honey, we did. Dad picked me up on the way." Mom smiled, and Tracy seemed to relax a bit.

A nurse came over and checked Julie's splint one final time, marking something on her clipboard. "Looks like you're good to go," she announced.

"Anybody hungry?" asked Dad, taking a deep breath and rubbing his hands together. "What do you say we head out and stop for pizza?"

"You mean it?" Julie asked. "Can I, Mom?"

"I mean all of us," Dad said. "It's been a rough day for everybody, and I think we could all use a break. What do you say?"

"I don't mind not cooking tonight," said Mom.

"And I can't do the dishes anyway!" said Julie,

pointing to her sling.

Julie looked over at Tracy, afraid she would refuse Dad's invitation. *Say yes, say yes,* Julie pleaded silently.

"I guess," said Tracy. "But only if we go to our old place in North Beach, so I can order the Very, Very Veggie pizza."

"Now, Tracy—" Mom started.

"It's okay," said Dad. "I don't mind driving us over there, then dropping you all back at your place. We can get two pizzas, so you can each choose your favorite. How about that?"

"Wow," said Julie, looking from Mom to Dad. "I should break my finger more often!"

THE BEST
THING EVER

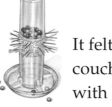

It felt funny to be home resting on the couch on a school day, playing Kerplunk with Mom all morning. Mom had told Julie she could stay home for a day, since it was Friday, and the doctor had recommended taking it easy for a few days.

With her uninjured left hand, Julie gingerly extracted a red stick from the marble-filled tower without upsetting a single marble. "Your turn, Mom," she said. "Bet you go *ker-plunk!*"

Mom smiled. "Honey, do you think we could finish the game later? I need to open the shop for at least a few hours today."

"You're not just saying that because you're about

to get clobbered, are you, Mom?" Julie teased.

"Boy, nothing gets past you," said Mom. "Now, will you be all right by yourself for a little while? I'm right downstairs if you need me. Come on down if you feel up to it."

"I should probably stay and work on my report. It's due on Monday. I have most of it on tape, but I haven't started writing it down yet. Hey, wait a minute—how am I going to write?" Julie asked, holding up her splinted finger. With all the adhesive tape wrapped around it, Julie thought it looked mummified.

"Hmm, that is going to be a problem," said Mom. "Do you want me to write a note to Ms. Hunter and ask if you can turn it in late?"

"I have a better idea," beamed Julie, jumping up off the sofa. "What if I could turn in my report on tape? I have a lot of it done that way, and I could finish it up without having to write anything.

"Sounds like a creative solution to me," said Mom. "And that way you won't fall behind. I'll call Ms. Hunter and talk to her about it Monday morning."

"Thanks, Mom," Julie said.

Julie spent the rest of the morning editing her

project, erasing certain parts of the tape (Tracy's telephone call about Matt) and adding in a few peppy introductions. "Coming up next: the exciting adventures of my dad, daredevil pilot Daniel Albright, when he was my same age. Hold on to your seats!"

Scanning down the list of topics for her project, Julie's finger stopped at the Best Thing That Ever Happened. She had planned to tell about the petition and getting onto the boys' basketball team. Momentarily, she was warmed by the memory of last night—being together as a family again, all four of them, the way it used to be. As if nothing had ever changed. Being a family again last night was possibly the Best Thing That Ever Happened. But if she were to include *that* in her report, it meant she would have to mention the Worst Thing.

When it came to the Worst Thing That Ever Happened, it seemed even harder to say the word *divorce* out loud onto a tape than to write it down. Julie turned on the tape recorder and pushed the record button. She held the microphone up to her face, but no words came.

"The worst thing that ever happened to me," Julie finally stammered, "was when . . ." She couldn't finish her sentence. Giving up, she pressed the stop button. *Great,* thought Julie. *Now I have to turn in a tape with nothing but air at the end.*

Feeling discouraged, Julie stared at her broken finger. Hey, wait a minute—breaking a finger was a bad thing that had happened to her. Not finishing the biggest basketball game of the season was a bad thing that had happened. Julie didn't even have to say a word about the divorce. Her broken finger could be the Worst Thing That Ever Happened.

Julie turned the tape player back on, pushed the record button, and held up the microphone. In a strong voice like a radio announcer, she told the whole story of the Best Thing Ever—the time she collected 150 signatures on a petition that convinced the principal and school board to let her play on the boys' basketball team. Then, for the Worst Thing Ever, she recounted the game against the Wildcats, complete with her trip to the hospital and her freakish Frankenstein of a finger.

Just as Julie was finishing up her tape, Tracy

came home from school. She plopped down on the sofa with her tennis racket.

"How was school today?" Julie started.

"You sound like Mom," said Tracy.

"No, I mean, didn't you have to turn in your science journal today?" Julie asked nervously.

"Yep. And guess what? I got an A. Even though my plant died."

Julie let out a small breath and sank back into the sofa with relief. "Tracy?" she said tentatively. "There's something I have to tell you."

Tracy set down her tennis racket. "What is it?"

"You know that time I watched your plant for you?" said Julie. "Well, I—um, I knocked it out the window by mistake. It was an accident, honest! I was afraid you'd be mad at me and flunk your assignment, so I got a new planter and tried to fix it."

"I know," said Tracy.

"You mean you knew all this time?"

Tracy cocked her head. "I figured you broke the pot. Did you really think I wouldn't be able to tell the difference between a hippo and a pig?"

"I guess not," said Julie in a small voice.

"Why didn't you just tell me what happened

instead of going to all that trouble to cover it up?"

Julie squirmed and looked down. "I'm sorry," she said finally. "Really, I am. I was going to tell you before you had to turn in your report, but when you were so mad at Dad yesterday for not being at the game and letting you down, I lost my nerve."

For a few moments, Tracy was quiet, and Julie was afraid her sister was angry. But when Tracy spoke, she just sounded sad. "I know I shouldn't have blown up at Dad. It wasn't his fault he wasn't at the game. But sometimes it's hard not to feel as if—well, as if he's let us down in a really big way. By leaving the family, I mean. By getting divorced." Tracy's voice quivered suddenly, and she turned away.

"But they *both* got divorced," Julie pointed out. "It wasn't just Dad; it was Mom, too. It's not fair to blame the whole thing on Dad."

Tracy was silent. When she turned back to Julie, her eyes were bright, and she blinked a few times to clear them. "You know it's important to tell the truth, Jules." She reached over and tweaked her sister's ponytail. "Besides, we're sisters, and sisters have to stick together. Promise me, next time you'll come talk to me and tell me?"

"Promise," said Julie. She hesitated a moment, then leaned forward and gave Tracy a hug.

On Monday morning, Julie was fumbling and trying to open her locker left-handed when T. J. saw her and called, "Hey, it's Cool Hand Albright. You're back! Let's see the big cast. My mom says you've got mettle, whatever that means."

Julie held up her splint for T. J. to see. "Oh, I've got *metal* all right! Broke my finger. It's not really a cast, just a splint. I'm like the Bionic Woman now."

"Oh, man," said T. J. "I can't believe Dunk ran you over."

"And I can't believe I had to miss the biggest game all season," said Julie. "Thanks for calling to tell me how the rest of the game went. I'm so bummed out we didn't win."

"But we came super close. Coach said we played our best game ever. We probably would have won if they hadn't injured our star player," T. J. teased.

"Thanks," said Julie with a smile. Taking a deep breath, she grabbed her tape recorder with her left

hand, slammed her locker shut, and headed for
Ms. Hunter's class, hurrying down the hall side
by side with T. J.

Everybody buzzed around Julie, talking about
the big game and Julie's broken finger. Like the
Telephone game, the story had grown with each
telling. One student had heard that Julie was rushed
to the hospital in an ambulance. Another had heard
that her finger got gangrene and had to be cut off!
Julie had not been this popular since the day her
mother had visited her class for Career Day and had
given everybody free bracelets and mood rings.

Ms. Hunter clapped her hands, and the students
returned to their seats to listen to one another's reports.

Angela went first. For the Worst Thing That
Ever Happened, she told about the time she jumped
into the pool and her bathing suit bottom came off.
The whole class burst out laughing, and Ms. Hunter
had to blink the lights just to get everybody to
settle down.

T. J. went next. He called his report "Cheaper by
the Half Dozen" and told all about living with five

sisters. (Julie couldn't imagine having five sisters—
one was plenty.) T. J. described how his mom gave
all the kids haircuts to save money. For the girls, she
just trimmed a few inches off the ends, but for T. J.,
she put a bowl on top of his head and cut off
all the hair below it. T. J. showed a picture of
himself in second grade, looking like Mo
from the Three Stooges.

"Now who's brave," Julie whispered when
T. J. sat down. "That took super-duper courage to
show everybody that picture!"

Finally, it was Julie's turn. Carrying her tape
recorder, she walked to the front of the class. "As
everybody knows, I broke my finger on my right
hand, so I couldn't write out my report in
handwriting," she started to explain.

"Aw, let's have a pity party," one of the students
remarked.

"Hey, my finger hurts too," somebody else
called out.

Julie laughed. "For real, I had to record my
report on tape. So I'm going to play it for you now."

The class listened intently to the stories of Dad's
big bike ride, Mom's runaway horse, Charlotte the

Spider Plant, and the Best Thing Ever—the petition and playing basketball for the Jaguars. Finally, Julie's voice on the tape said, "And last but not least, I'm going to tell you about the Worst Thing That Ever Happened."

Click. Julie turned off the tape recorder.

"Hey, no fair!" said a boy in the back row. "You have to let us hear the worst thing. That's the best part!"

Julie looked hesitantly at her teacher. She could feel her palms beginning to sweat, yet her throat felt dry as chalk dust. "Ms. Hunter," she said, trying to swallow, "would it be okay if I just tell the last part aloud, I mean, without the tape? I sort of changed my mind about what I want to say."

"I don't see that as a problem," said Ms. Hunter.

Julie straightened up her slumped shoulders and began. "I was going to play back the story of my broken finger for the Worst Thing That Ever Happened to me," she explained. "But really, that wouldn't be telling the truth. Because even worse than a broken finger is when my family broke apart. A few months ago, my mom and dad decided to get a divorce. That means I don't get to live with both of my parents anymore."

Julie's stomach turned somersaults. She wanted to leave to go get a drink of water, but she forced her feet to stand steady.

"When I broke my finger," she continued, "my mom and dad both came to the hospital. And after I got bandaged up, we all went out for pizza together. I was so happy to have us all back together again that it was almost worth breaking my finger. Except that it only lasted for one night. We weren't together again for real, permanently." Julie paused, thinking what to say next. This time the class was dead quiet, waiting for her to continue.

Julie knew she had covered all the topics for her report, but she realized there was still something she was trying to say. "Just now, as I was playing back the tape, I remembered something my dad told me when he broke his foot. He said that a broken bone heals back together even stronger than before it was broken."

Julie's stomach was feeling less queasy, and her voice was stronger now, more confident. "I think families are kind of like bones—they can break too, but in some ways, it makes you even stronger. And when one person's in trouble or gets hurt, families pull together, and you can still count on them to be there for you.

"The end. That's the Story of My Life. So far."

Everybody clapped. Julie walked down the aisle, back to her seat at the initial-carved desk she'd come to think of as her own. Her heart still pounding, she slid into her chair, aware now of the pulsing in her injured finger. She knew in her heart that the break in her family would always be there. But the love she felt for her sister and her parents, and the love they felt for her, was as strong as ever. That part couldn't be broken.

LOOKING BACK

SCHOOL
IN THE
1970s

A classroom in the 1970s

If you could step back in time and go to school with Julie Albright, your classroom would look pretty much the same as classrooms today: same type of lockers, same gym, same cafeteria—even the same plastic trays and slightly overcooked food! But gradually, you'd notice some differences. When the teacher passes out a worksheet, which she calls a *ditto*, it's printed in a funny purple color instead of black and white. Your classmates never use calculators to do their math. Rather than showing an educational video or DVD, the teacher shows a *filmstrip*,

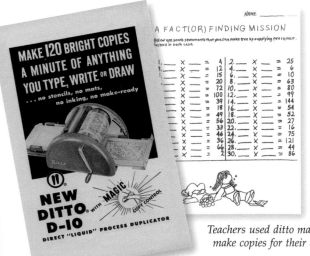

Teachers used ditto machines to make copies for their students.

a series of still images with a voice-over narration. And there are no computers anywhere in the school.

When Julie was growing up, computers, calculators, photocopiers, and VCRs had all been invented and were used by businesses, but they were too expensive for schools to use. Students didn't even learn how to type until they were in high school, like Tracy, and then only if they wanted to. Many people who grew up in the 1970s wish they had taken typing in school back then, because their poor typing skills make it much harder for them to use a computer today.

typewriter

This magazine article showed teachers ways to use plants as teaching tools.

Despite the differences in technology, teachers in Julie's time were just as creative as they are today. One teaching approach that had become very popular by the 1970s was *hands-on* learning, or learning by doing rather than just by reading a textbook. The hands-on approach, which is still the norm today, included every-thing from science experiments and field trips to student projects like Julie's "Story of My Life" report and Tracy's plant project.

Students doing hands-on experiments in science class

THE JOLLY GREEN CLASSROOM

81

A major goal of American schools in the 1970s was to provide equal opportunities for all students—for students with disabilities, for gifted students, for girls and boys, for black students and white students. Congress passed new laws to make sure all students had access

Schools started having students of all races and abilities learn together.

to good school programs and resources. These laws led to many changes: Girls could play on sports teams. Gifted students could take accelerated or enrichment classes. Students with disabilities or special needs received extra support.

This New Jersey girl was on the junior varsity football team at her high school.

Perhaps the biggest challenge was to equalize the education of black and white students. Schools in black communities were usually poorer than schools in neighboring white communities. They sometimes didn't have enough books or even desks for all the students. To fix this inequality, cities sought to *integrate* the schools, so that a mix of black students and white students would attend. Cities began

There's nothing like a long bus ride together for making new friends!

busing some students to schools outside their
neighborhoods, enabling black students to attend
formerly all-white schools and vice versa.

Not everyone liked the busing. Some parents didn't
want their kids spending long hours on a bus. Children
often felt connected to their neighborhood schools and
didn't want to attend school far away in an unknown
neighborhood. And some communities simply didn't
agree with the goal of integration. In a few cities, most
notably Boston,
busing protests
grew violent.

*Police sometimes
escorted school
buses to prevent
problems from
protestors.*

...ts Top Tory

Alioto Gives Big Tax Rate 'Fat Chance'

Jerry Burns

Immediate Cut

S.F. Schools End Sports Programs

In San Francisco, the busing went smoothly, but the schools faced another serious problem: they were running out of money. In early 1975, the San Francisco school district canceled most sports and after-school programs to save money. So a local music promoter, Bill Graham, put on a benefit concert in Golden Gate Park called SNACK, for "Students Need Athletics, Culture, and Kicks." Famous rock bands and musicians including Bob Dylan, the Grateful Dead, Joan Baez, and Santana, donated their talents to the cause. The all-day concert was a major event for the community and raised $170,000 for the school district. Because the concert was to help the schools, many high-school students attended.

Today, benefit rock concerts are quite common, but in Julie's time they were a new idea— one of the many creative solutions people found to address social problems in the 1970s.

A SNEAK PEEK AT

HAPPY NEW YEAR,
Julie

*Julie enjoy's helping Ivy's family prepare for Chinese
New Year —until a shopping trip in Chinatown
takes a turn for the worse.*

As Julie and Ivy joined the throngs of people crowding the streets, Julie's eyes grew wide with wonder. She had been to Chinatown before, but today the neighborhood was like a city unto itself, bursting with new colors, smells, and sounds. Sidewalk vendors called out in Chinese, their voices dipping and rising like songbirds as they unloaded produce from trucks. Silvery fish stared out of wooden crates labeled with Chinese characters. Racks of bright silks fluttered in the breeze, while lines of laundry flapped from second-story balconies.

The children followed Mrs. Ling up and down Stockton Street. Elbow to elbow, they threaded their way through the crowds, past cardboard boxes brimming with wrinkly vegetables and prickly fruits.

"What are all these?" asked Julie.

"Chinese cabbage, wood ear mushrooms, and bitter melon," Ivy told her, pointing at each vegetable.

"How are you ever going to eat all this?" asked Julie as Ivy's mom began to load them up with bags of food.

"Don't worry, we will," said Ivy. "Chinese New Year lasts for fifteen days! It starts on New Year's Eve with a big family dinner at home. It ends with a feast at the Happy Panda on the night of the dragon parade—"

"—which *I'm* going to be in!" Andrew piped up. "And it's time for me to go to practice. See you later!"

"No fair," said Ivy. "We need you to help carry bags!"

"That's what you have Julie for," Andrew teased, waving and heading off toward the Chinatown Y.

"We can't forget tangerines, for good luck," Ivy told Julie. "Look for tangerines that still have stems with leaves attached. "That's for friendship, and staying connected."

Julie carefully selected a tangerine with a firm stem and two green leaves. She thought about her own family, about Tracy and Dad. *If only it were that easy to stay connected.*

Soon Julie and Ivy were weighed down with pink plastic bags brimming with fruits and vegetables. Mrs. Ling piled them even higher with peach blossoms, peonies, and chrysanthe mums.

"Peach blossoms are for long life and good luck, too," Ivy said.

"We need good luck," said Julie. "Good luck carrying all this stuff home!"

Mrs. Ling paused outside a souvenir shop to talk to a woman in a red quilted jacket. Ivy and Julie set their bags down, waiting while the women spoke rapidly in Chinese.

"Hey, Ivy, is the doll shop anywhere around here?" Julie asked, looking up and down the street.

"It's just past the kite shop, a few doors down."

"Do we have time to look in the window?"

"Sure," said Ivy, glancing at her mother and the souvenir-shop lady. "They'll be talking for about a million years."

Pushing through the crowds, the girls gazed into the storefront window. "Wow," said Julie. "They have doll dresses and dollhouses and miniature furniture. Let's go inside!"

A bell jangled as they opened the door. The shop was like an attic crammed full of treasure. Jade princess dolls. Dragon tea sets, drums, and fans. Traditional Chinese papercuts. Lion masks and lanterns. Satin dresses and pajamas.

"Look," said Ivy. "They have Chinese dresses in girls' sizes. Let's try them on."

Julie lifted a turquoise dress from the rack that looked very much like Yue Yan's dress. It felt silky-smooth to the touch. "If I had a dress this fancy, I'd ask Dad to take me back to the Fairmont Hotel. Only this time, Tracy wouldn't be there to ruin it."

Ivy selected a red dress like Li Ming's. "If I had a dress this fancy, I'd wear it for New Year's!" she said.

The girls tugged the dresses on over their clothes. They whirled and twirled in front of the long mirror.

"Wish to buy?" asked the saleslady, smiling and nodding.

"Not today, thank you," Ivy said politely.

The girls reluctantly hung the dresses up and hurried back outside. They ran past the kite shop, a Chinese bakery, and an herb shop. But when they got to the souvenir shop, Mrs. Ling and Missy were nowhere in sight. Even their bags were gone.

Ivy and Julie looked up and down the sidewalk, inside the souvenir shop, and across the street. "Mama!" Ivy called out, trying to see above the crowd. "Mama! Where are you?"

*The girls tugged the dresses on over their clothes. They
whirled and twirled in front of the long mirror.*

"It's my fault," said Julie frantically. "We shouldn't have gone inside that shop. We took too long. They could be anywhere!"

"But Mama wouldn't leave without us!" Ivy went back into the souvenir shop to ask the shopkeeper if she knew which way her mother and sister had gone. The woman replied in rapid Chinese. Ivy's face fell.

"She says they went to find us," she told Julie.

"Okay," said Julie, taking a deep breath. "Think, Ivy, if your mom was looking for us, where would she go?"

Ivy closed her eyes for a minute. "I know! She must have gone to the fortune-cookie factory. Remember? She said that was her last stop."

"Do you know how to get there?" Julie asked.

"It can't be too far from here. I know it's in a little alley, next to a barbershop. C'mon. Hurry!"

Julie and Ivy bent low and ducked through the crowds filling the sidewalk. When they turned the corner, the crowds thinned out a bit. They rushed down a few blocks, searching in every direction. Nothing looked familiar. Julie's heart quickened. She felt lost in a foreign country. Even the words people spoke were impossible to understand.

Ivy made a sharp turn into an alley where the tall backs of buildings blocked the sunlight. A cascade of overturned boxes littered the alley. Heaps of cabbage leaves were scattered every which way.

"Pee-yew! This place smells!" Julie held her nose. "Are you sure this is it?"

"No," said Ivy, her voice cracking. "I'm not sure."

"Let's try the next alley," said Julie. Somehow, as long as they kept moving, it didn't seem so scary.